STORY BY **Douglas Wood**   ILLUSTRATIONS BY **Elly M. Van Diest**

Chickadee's Message

To Diane

With every good wish...

5/09

Adventure Publications, Inc.
Cambridge, MN

DEDICATION

To all who are "bright of eye and strong of heart," like the Chickadee—or would like to be—Douglas Wood

Dedicated to Bill with love and unending support and encouragement of my art, and to my children with special thanks—Elly Van Diest

Illustrated by Elly Van Diest

Cover and book design by Jonathan Norberg
Edited by Brett Ortler

10 9 8 7 6 5 4 3 2 1
Copyright 2009 by Douglas Wood
Published by Adventure Publications, Inc.
820 Cleveland Street South
Cambridge, MN 55008
1-800-678-7006
www.adventurepublications.net
Printed in China

ISBN-13: 978-1-59193-228-4
ISBN-10: 1-59193-228-9

IT HAS LONG BEEN SAID among the ancient peoples of the north woods and prairies that the Chickadee, though very small, is very wise. This brave and cheerful little creature understands many of the mysteries at the heart of nature, and in the hearts of humans. There is an old story that tells of these things . . .

In the dim and distant days of the Long Ago, the Human Beings were very young, just beginning to learn how to live upon the earth.

But they looked and listened well. They learned from their relatives, the birds and the animals and the plants. They learned that the earth was good, full of many teachers and wise helpers who showed the People a good path to walk. Thus they learned to survive, to live in balance and in beauty.

But this was also a time when the evil powers struggled fiercely to over-come the good. The evil powers were not pleased to see the People learn-ing to live so happily upon the earth. So they decided to try to discourage the People, to make them lose heart. Perhaps even to destroy them.

And so it was that the evil powers sent cold and bitter winds, snow and storms to try to break the People's spirit. They sent heat and drought and times of famine. They sent floods to try to wash the People away, and fires that sometimes swept through the forests and over the prairies.

The evil powers set all these forces loose upon the earth, to create hardship for the People.

Finally they said, "Surely by now we have broken the will of the Human Beings. It is time to send a messenger to learn how things are with them and to bring word back to us."

And so it was they called upon
Chickadee, a very small bird, but
bright of eye and strong of heart.
Chickadee had well-survived all
the storms and hardships that
had been loosed upon the earth.

Now the evil powers called the
little bird into their lodge. They
gave their instructions and sent
him on his mission to the People.

It was not easy for Chickadee to find his way through the winds and storms, through cold and darkness. But the little bird was wise, knew where to find food and to seek shelter.

At night he rested in the cavities of old trees, or deep within the sheltering boughs of spruces or cedars.

Finally he found his way to the dwellings of the People.

There, he was treated with kindness and respect, and given a place of honor by the fireside to warm himself. He was given food and anointed with a smudge of fat, the sign of plenty. He was marked with a dab of red paint, symbol of the mystery of life.

After these ceremonies and marks of respect, the People waited and listened patiently to learn why their little guest had come.

When Chickadee had explained his mission, his hosts held council and formulated a reply for their messenger to take back to those who had sent him. This is what they said:

"Go back to the evil powers, Little Brother, and tell them this: that the Human Beings are still alive and hopeful and ever will be; that the People will not be broken by discouragement, nor defeated by storms and stress, nor vanquished by hunger, nor destroyed by hardship. Tell them that the Human Beings will always live upon the earth, that we will remember the goodness of life, and that the world is filled with beauty."

This is the message that Chickadee brought back to the evil powers. It is the message these little birds have proclaimed ever since, from firs and pines and oaks and cottonwoods, in winter and in summer, in blizzard and in drought.

It is why, after many generations, there is still a special bond of affection between Human Beings and the Chickadee.

And it is why, to this day, to hear a Chickadee is to feel just a little braver, a tiny bit stronger, and to feel the gentle tug of a smile upon one's face.

MANY YEARS AGO, on a solo canoe trip in the North Woods, I was having a bad day. Rather, a whole series of them. I'd been going through a rough patch personally, and now a combination of poor luck and worse weather had me lonesome and in a deep blue mood. As I paddled in wind-driven sleet and rain, I passed under an overhanging spruce. "Chick-a-dee-dee-dee" came the sound. And there was the tiny black-masked bandit, hanging upside-down, pecking merrily at a spruce cone. Though I had seen countless chickadees in my life, it was as though I were now seeing one for the very first time. He called again and another answered, and another. And I saw that the whole tree was alive with chickadees, behaving as they always do, active, cheerful, indomitable, enjoying life and the beautiful weather.

After staring for a good, long time, I wondered—what happens if a chickadee gets depressed? I realized I didn't think I'd ever seen a depressed chickadee. Then I remembered that many other small bird species like to hang around with chickadees. Good survival skills, perhaps? People enjoy their company as well. Just good survival skills? Good cheer? Good company? Strong spirit? And then I thought . . . maybe it's all a part of the same thing. Whether or not ornithologists would agree with my analysis, I paddled away a little stronger, with a brighter outlook that I've kept, despite ups and downs, ever since. And when the weather of life turns foul, there is always a little black-bibbed friend in the back of my mind, reminding me . . .

Years later, I first found a version of this ancient tale in a delightful old book (Prairie Smoke, by Melvin R. Gilmore, Columbia University Press, 1929) and got a shiver up my spine. It was part of a long, rich tradition of stories about the chickadee among Native American peoples. I realized that I was just one in a long history of people who learned something special from this dauntless ball of fluff. And I felt, in a powerful new way, more connected to the natural world and to people everywhere. I have been telling this story, and others like it, ever since. And I am delighted to share it here, beautifully brought to life with illustrations by Elly Van Diest, and presented with love and care by Adventure Publications.

To all who take it to heart and grasp its meanings: Good Journey.

DW

BLACK-CAPPED CHICKADEE

The Black-Capped Chickadee is a little bird with a big personality that often visits backyards across the northern United States and Canada. A frequent visitor to bird feeders, it often swoops down quickly and hops from place to place as it pecks seeds. Unlike many other birds, the Chickadee doesn't migrate in winter and needs to feed every day in winter. Yet rain, snow or shine, the Chickadee always seems to stay cheerful and lively, going along on its merry way, storing seeds and coming back for them later. In fact, a single Chickadee can store food in thousands of different hiding places and can remember many of them. Some studies even suggest that a Chickadee's brain actually gets larger when it is hiding seeds and gets smaller when food is more plentiful.

The Chickadee's name comes from its familiar "chika-dee-dee-dee-dee" call, but it also gives a high-pitched, two-toned "fee-bee" call. The Chickadee's call might sound simple, but its calls are complex and language-like. Chickadees are quite chatty too; they can have as many as 15 different calls. These calls include all sorts of information; some calls identify different flocks while others alert other Chickadees to predators.

Despite the harsh environment they live in and the dangers they often face, Chickadees are revered, in part, because of their curiosity. The Chickadee is naturally inquisitive, and it's often easy to feed them by hand. Perhaps it's this plucky spirit, coupled with its boundless energy and persistence, that makes the Chickadee universally beloved.

DOUGLAS WOOD has been called Minnesota's "renaissance man" – author, artist, musician, naturalist, wilderness guide. As a writer of books for children and adults he has almost two million copies in print, including the classics Old Turtle and Grandad's Prayers of the Earth. Among his many honors and awards have been the Christopher Medal, ABBY Award, International Reading Association Book of the Year, Minnesota Book Award, Midwest Publishers Association Book of the Year, Parent's Choice Award, Barnes and Noble Star of the North, and World Story Telling Award.

ELLY MATTSON VAN DIEST is an artist and illustrator who specializes in watercolors. Her paintings are widely held in private and public collections. A native Minnesotan, former public school teacher and graphic designer for the Great River Regional Library system, she lives in a "century" home near the Mississippi River in St. Cloud, Minnesota.